WINNIE UMBRELLA PUBLISHING PRESENTS
And Then He said
What would you have done differently?
Vanessa Y

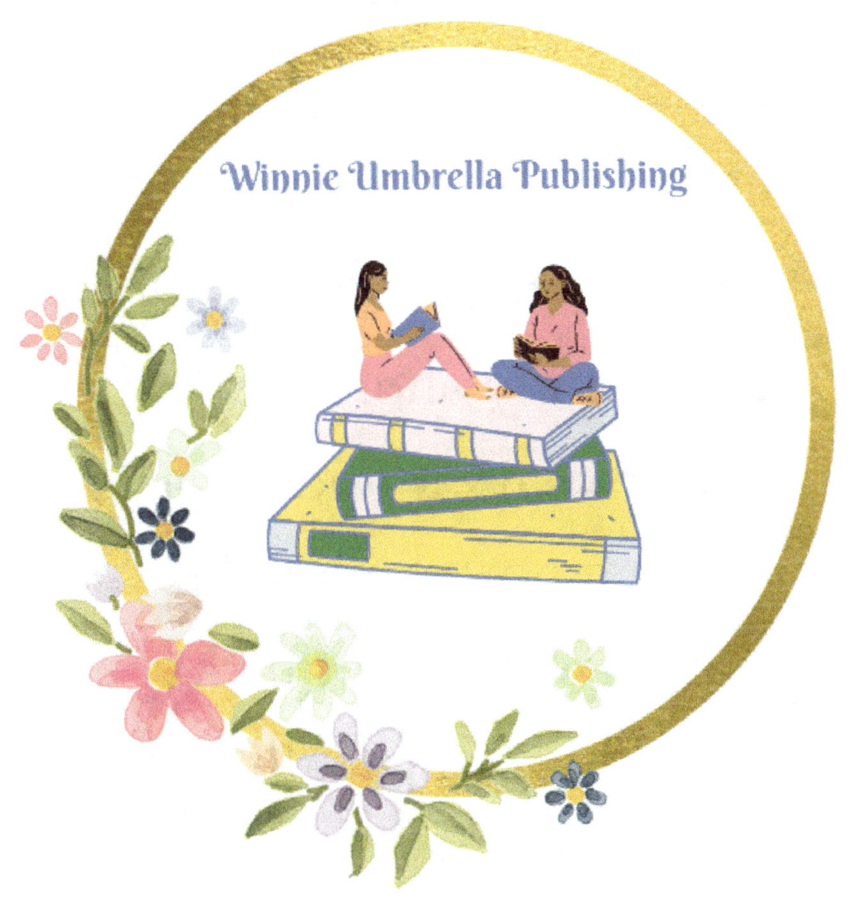


Copyright © 2024 Vanessa Y




ISBN: 978-1-7379337-6-2

Thank you, for choosing to read my short story. I appreciate it and hope you enjoy the laughs, plot twist, and quirky moments. Hopefully you join the other adventures of this character as I enjoy writing them. Don't forget to share the laughter with a friend.

Vanessa Y

# Chapter 1

## Where do I Begin?

I fell in love with a friend, but I didn't know why. He was so different from all the other men I knew; but he was just another guy. I followed his body language and words to a "T." That's when I knew "Bitch I was fucking crazy." Sitting here laughing, I have to tell you how it started. Just so you can see how I thought I may or may not been crazy. You be the judge.

Picture this it's 2018, I just moved to Atlanta, Georgia coming from South Carolina; I didn't know anyone. Ya'll, I had to leave South Carolina. You know it was the same old mindset and same old men. Not to sound bitter, but that was what I was around. I didn't fit in with the Drama by day; cheating by night mentality so, I moved. You know the change your surroundings to get a different outcome. Don't get me wrong; I miss my friends and family, but I just wanted something different. So, Atlanta it was.

The last relationship I was in really secured my mindset to move away. Let me take you back to 2016. I was in a relationship with this buster named Keith. He had a good job, all his teeth, and could eat away all your problems if you know what I mean.

We had been dating for 1 year and long story short he was full of shit. You know what I am going to tell you the story that really put a big STOP in that train wreck. It was our one-year anniversary and being the loving girlfriend, I was I wanted to decorate his apartment to celebrate. I had a key and everything.  I also hired a massage therapist to help him relax coming home from work, so I had to let her in a little early to set up her equipment.

I get there and yes you may have guessed it.... I caught him on the couch fucking another woman. I grabbed the first thing I could and clocked him on the side of his head. Then chased the other woman as she locked herself in the bathroom. She looked familiar, but everything was going on so fast.

As I kicked on his bathroom door; he grabbed his clothes. The massage therapist left ya'll, but she came back. Apparently, she put all of her equipment back in her truck. She was definitely a real one and didn't even know me. I still paid her just out of the circumstances of went down, but back to my story. While I'm screaming at the door "This ain't the Players Club, come out Ebony." Keith was still over there trying to regain his balance. The familiar chick never came out the bathroom. As Keith came wobbling towards me with that, "Baby I'm sorry mumbo jumbo.

Keith, "She was just helping me with your gifts!"

This negro thinks I'm stupid. As I brought my fist up to punch him, he kept saying something. I didn't know or cared what he said, I wanted to get another lick in before the cops got called.

The massage therapist who now has her hair tied in a bun and was guarding the door screamed listen to him. In the mist of the chaos it got quiet. Keith was trying to catch his breath.

And then he said, "She was my cousin, she didn't mean anything, she was just helping out with your gifts."

Pause his nasty rant, but that's why she looked so familiar to me. I met his family at the cookout a few months ago. I saw her, her mama, and everything. She was his legitimate cousin. Just nasty.

I screamed, "You Nasty Bitch, "I'm telling EVERYBODY!"

Mark my words I did exactly that. My revenge was exposing that ass. I Facebook Live everything and it went viral. Crazy part is a lot of people didn't see nothing wrong with that nasty stuff. So, like I said same mindset, same Ol type of men; so, I moved.

Fast Forward to Now.

# Chapter 2
# Tonight Was New

On this particular Friday night, I'm sitting in my new apartment bored as fuck. I don't mind it, but my neighbors are kicking it hard, blasting music, the works. I kind of wish they would invite me though. As I sat on my couch, and I started scrolling meet up sites to just get out the house. Being 26 in Atlanta has been cool so far; but I haven't indulged in the night life just yet. My new job is ok, but I can tell that I will not be there a full year. I am already looking for another position. Them hoes are too messy for me. I haven't even been there for 3 days, but that's another story. I am a Registered Nurse so work wouldn't be so hard to find.

So, while I'm scrolling, I found the perfect event for me to go to. It also was a few blocks from my apartment.

I jumped up Yelling, "Boom Bitch I'm going!"

As I walked to my closet, I second guessed that idea. I have only been in the ATL for a few weeks, so I haven't gone out to add some spice to my style. Here goes doubt creeping in so I started my way back to the couch.

As I walked down my hallway, I almost fell on Maxine ball. Maxine is my Gerbil. Yes, I named her after the Living Single Character. She was strong, funny, beautiful & confident. Regaining my balance, I asked myself what would Maxine do? I went back to my closet and grabbed my sexiest outfit. A simple two-piece orange fitted dress. Baby this outfit looks too good on me. After that Keith drama I worked out a lot and that made me extra fine. I got everything I needed especially, my pepper spray and lipstick taser. Ya'll need to get you one.

My apartments are a mix of young and under 40 vibes. I'm not saying I get over dressed to take out the trash, but I do look casual cute when I do. (Flips Hair)

So let me give you the visual. I'm looking good in my outfit makeup / hair everything is on point. Oh, and my perfume is on the fruity side.

Back to my story. I'm walking to my car and see that I'm blocked in by this 2018 Candy Paint Red with the gloss Hellcat.
I'm yelling to the air at this point, "Now ain't this a bitch. Who in the drug dealer, 3 baby mamas, car is this?"
The car was on, and no one was in it. At that moment it looked like I was the only one outside or so I thought.

As I continued to say everything about the owner of that car; A strong deep voice came up from behind me.

The car owner, "My Bad Lovvvvvvve."

Before the Love could get out of his mouth; I jumped so quick, turned around and jabbed that lipstick taser into his neck.

That man dropped so quick. I'm so scared that I didn't know if I should run or help him. First off, he should not have been that close to me. Thoughts kept flooding my head. As I started to come to my senses; I started to look around. Either the goons or the 3 baby mamas coming out of somewhere. Now I have to fight. The guy let out a groan sound. That brought me back to reality.

Hesitantly I said, "I'm sorry you scared me." While I was helping him up. Ya'll I know it sounds mean, but he was too damn heavy for me to lift up. He still twitched a little as I leaned him up against my car.

The streetlights was on so it gave me a good view of his face. Damn he was fine. I mean smooth skin, white pearly teeth, outfit and all. He started to catch his breath. All I could think of was how he gone cuss me out, which I was going to tase his ass again. I DON'T PLAY THAT, but he didn't. This nigga crazy. He just laughed in-between catching his breath. I stepped back, because I be damned if he gets a chance to grab me. While still holding his neck he apologizes for scaring me. The irony of him apologizing and I'm the one who tased him.

The car guy, "I see I'm in your way let me move my car."

He got into his car and rolled his window down. And then he said.

The car guy, "Since you tried to 187 me, let's make amends and I take you to go get something to eat. Just so you know who I am and this won't happen again."

I didn't know if it was the dress, being fresh meat, or dude was trying to kill me. One thing I did know it was a Hell to the Nawll for me; plus he was too fine. Trouble fine, different women every hour fine and they are ok with it. Also, sprung over some dick fine. Don't judge me, I brushed up against that "Thang" when I tried to lean him up on my car. I said no in the most direct way possible. He just smiled.

The car guy, "I won't hold you up, but my name is Trey. What's yours?"

Can you guess what my response was? I had to keep up with the weirdness of the night and told that man my name is, "Taser!" He laughed while driving off and holding his neck. I hopped in my car so fast, locked the door, and prayed y'all. I didn't want no deaths on me and damn sholl didn't want to fight any baby mamas tomorrow. Either way if they did come they was going to get these thunder cookies.

If you don't know what Thunder Cookies your childhood was nothing like mines. It means these hands, that Clap Clap, but back to my story.

Me praying, "Please Lord don't let that man, he said his name was Trey to be hurt and die from my actions towards him. Please let this night be filled with laughter and fun. If there is some drama coming around me or towards me; please let me make a safe exit home without being involved or the cause of it. Thank you in advance ❤️."

The way the evening was going, and I haven't even left my apartments yet; I had to make sure I was covered with God protection. It was about 10:20pm, so I took a few deep breaths and headed to the event. Y'all thought that I was going to let that little distraction stop me; nope it did not. My plans were to be back home at least by 12:30am. I just wanted to see what the vibe was like out here in Atlanta.

# Chapter 3
# Lets Party

Since the event was only a few blocks away, I made it before it hit 10:39pm. It was definitely a sight. The parking lot was packed, there was food trucks, and everything. I squeezed my car right beside one too. Whoever did this setup is a genius. The bouncers were in swimwear, straight eye candy for men and women. It's October so this was way different to me. As I walk inside, I noticed everyone kind of dressed the same. Labeled brands from head to toe, see through outfits, the works. Glitz and glamour at a beach theme event, different but okay I'm observing. I stood out and that's not a bad thing. Dressing sexy simple tonight worked in my favor. As I was walking to the bar with my hips moved to the beat of the music. I could see the women rolling their eyes and feel the stare of the men.

The walk to the bar felt a little too long. I was getting too tired throwing these hips. As I waited for a bartender to come over to take my drink order; I started listening to the conversations around me. Y'all need to try it sometime. I tried not to laugh at the man next to me trying to start a tab with a Walmart gift card. He looked really drunk and had on the latest overpriced designers. The bartender finally deaded the conversation with Mr. Gift Card and took my drink order.

Bartender, "What would you like?"

"Can you make your signature drink.", I replied. She smiled and came back with this colorful drink that taste like happiness. If you don't know what happiness taste like; dance around to your favorite song. I sparked up a conversation with the bartender. Her name was Sidney. She was gorgeous and apparently makes a lot of money a night doing her job.

I wished her all the best and stayed at the bar awhile until that drink kicked in. I can see why Mr. Gift Card was so drunk. That one drink crept all the way up on me. I will definitely get some water before I get another one of those happiness drinks. I had to rush to the restroom because that drink was going right through me. Moving through the thick crowd was annoying; you couldn't see the walls and I didn't know where I was going. The ignorance popped off like it does at all events and a fight breaks out. I'm trying to go around all that mess to find the restroom. Someone bumped me so hard to the point I thought; alright I'm going to pee myself and no one would know. With all that commotion going on they wouldn't think twice just a spilled drink. Getting deeper in the crowd I got bumped again and fell right into the arms of "Dante". He looked down and smiled.

Dante, "Are you good?"

Me, "Yes now I am. Oh do you know where the restroom is?"

Dante was still holding me as he walked me to the restroom. You would've thought we was a couple. We finally made it and by my surprise it was clean. Public restrooms make me cringe, but that's beside the point. He was still waiting on me at the door. At this point the liquor had kicked in. I smiled at him.

Me, "So you waited?"

And then he said.

Dante, "Yes I couldn't let my new friend get hurt out here with all this drama going on. Let me at least walk you half way back to your man."

I laughed so hard because he was so smooth with it. He was a good 6 foot 3 inches tall, and you could tell he worked out. Sexy slim with one key earring in his ear and lips LL Cool J would be jealous of. I had him to walk me back to the bar. As we walked everyone stopped him. Men and women. I clearly put together he was the host of this event.

This was one night I got to tell my homegirls back home. I went from almost catching a case in the parking lot with Trey to mingling with the host of a really big event. When we made it to the bar, we talked for the rest of the time I was there. He even got my real name which is Trinity. I really was having fun then I looked at my phone and it was 3 in the morning. Time definitely flew by. I didn't have to go home but I didn't want to be out super late either. So, I got Dante number and the bartender Sydney number as I headed out. Dante offered to walk me to my car which I didn't mind. This was his event, and he took the time to walk me to my car. Straight gentleman. I was definitely feeling him. We made it to my car, and he gave me a strong hug. Those sexy tatted arms of his picked me up off the ground and leaned me close so he could breathe in my scent. While he still had me in the air, he buried his nose in my neck. His lips barely rested on my neck.

Dante, "You smell so good. Like some warm peaches. Call me so I know you made it home. I can't wait to see you again."
It felt so good being in his arms. The level of closeness without the pressure of sex was so alluring. I wouldn't be mad if we started kissing, but we didn't. He slowly let me down so I could feel all what he was working with. I got in my car and slowly drove away watching him in the rear-view mirror as he walked back to the event. Side note, maybe I was too focused on him that I didn't notice it was three guys with him. Maybe they stood back to protect our privacy, but they walked back in with him. Red Flag number 1. I need to watch out for that next time I see him. I was definitely going to see him again. When I made it home, I called Dante, he answered and then switched to a video call. Remind you it's almost 4 in the morning now. His event is still going on strong. More people came after I left. This is definitely a new nightlife I have to get use to.

When the video popped up of Donte all I could see was some beautiful teeth. I love a good smile; that's my weakness. He stepped to the backroom and we had a 5 minute conversation. He told me to get some rest and then hung up. I was in a strong like, lust, or whatever for this man. He was definitely on the top of my list of he can get it. Doesn't mean it would happen but he's on there.

# Chapter 4
# 6 Months Later

Fast forward 6 months later. I am still at that job with them messy hoes. I did land a job at Emory hospital that starts in a few weeks. It's paying twice as much as I'm making now. Blessings on Blessings. I ran into Trey a few times after that parking lot incident. I didn't have to use my Taser or anything. He was actually nice. It was a short encounter, but each time he would hold his neck, shake his hand and laugh. I still haven't figured out who he was coming over this way to see. I'm still seeing Donte, but on a friend level. We have been skating, to the movies, I met his friends, even his uncle. It has been all fun and games. As his friend we haven't kissed or had sex. He has though held me right in his arms when it's time for me to leave him. The romance was definitely there for me. I was falling for him. Tripping and all.

I'm known as Donte "TT". Where the heck that nick name came from, I don't know. Oh, and that bartender Sydney; she is my closest friend here. I'm really grateful to have met her. She does side eye Donte though. Nothing bad she just says he has hoes. At this point I'm his friend so she doesn't want me to get caught up in that. I also met a few other women that I occasionally hang out with to get away from that Donte TT social group sometimes. Looking back now I'm happy I did that, but everything around me at that moment was going good.

# Chapter 5
# Sundress Season

The change up was real. Let's start with Trey. It was around April and sundress season was starting for me. Remind you when I go take the trash out, I look casual cute. It was one of those days to be cute. So, before I went to take the trash out, I put Maxine into her ball so she could run around. The trash dispenser is 3 buildings down so the walk was a nosey lady heaven. I put my Air pods in my ears to not be disturbed but I was definitely listening to my surroundings. One building is where it seems like someone is always moving in and out. Another building you hear kids playing loud. The building by the trash dispenser is where the weed at. The smell is so strong like it's a damn dispensary. Nice neighbors though. Someone always cooking and today it smells like cookies.

As I continued with my walk, I heard someone say, "Hey Taser." I tried not to pause and act like I heard it. Hench the air pods in my ear. I finally made it to the Trash dispenser, threw my trash away, and pulled out my hand sanitizer. I turned around and boom there he was. He was looking good with his ugly self.

Trey, "Hey Taser, so you just gone ignore me calling your name?"

Yes, I am petty, so I was like, "What you say? I had my Air Pods in?"

He smiled and then he said, "Why you out here taking out the trash? Your man hands broke or some?"

Trinity, "Bruh I am more than capable of taking out the trash, run the world, and look beautiful while doing it.

I made sure to stand with my hands on my hip to emphasize my sundress hitting every curve on my body. ATL has been feeding me good. Trey stood there smiling.

Trey, "Yes you are Queen that can do anything she wants, but Queens also needs nourishment. Are you hungry?"

Am I hungry Hecks yeah, but that's not his business. Let me relax and be nice.

Trinity, "I can eat."

He motioned for me to follow him to his car. I let him know that I have to go home and wash my hands; plus get my purse. He said I didn't need it, but I still went and got it though. If anything goes down, I have my Taser with me. Soon as we got to my apartment, he tried to be a gentleman and open my door. Maxine rolled her ass right out the door. Trey gone scream, "You got some big ass rats." The words "Boy Fuck You" echoed as I ran after Maxine.

"Help me get her", I yelled while chasing her. Remind you he thinks this is a rat, and my dress didn't give me any luck into catching her either. Unless I pull this dress up to catch her and that was a big NO.

Don't judge me, but I didn't have any panties on. That also didn't stop me from chasing her though. Luckily Trey caught her before she hit the parking lot. He laughed all the way back to my apartment.

Trey, "So you got a Gerbil?"

Trinity, "Yes."

Trey, "What's its name?"

I grabbed her and said, "Maxine Shaw."

Trey, "All because she's a boss."

Trinity, "Exactly." The fact he knew that goes together made me smile on the low.

I grabbed my purse, put Maxine in her luxury cage then washed my hands. As I headed out with Trey it felt different.

# Chapter 6
## A Moment with Trey

Getting into that 2018 Hellcat was kind of cool. He didn't drive crazy, and it was like the butterflies came out to greet us at every red light. He took me to one of his favorite diners called Copycat Burgers. The name sounded crazy, but the food smelled really good. We sat in a booth near the middle of the diner. Not too close to the front door or the restroom. Perfect spot to see the food being made and to get a cute glow from the sun glare at the window. After the waiter took our order and left Trey leaned in towards me.

Trey, "So you got a Gerbil."

Trinity, "Yes I do, are you hating?"

Trey, "Nawll that's different. I like that. You know anytime I'm around you, I'm doing something out of my ordinary flow."

The waiter walked back with our food.

The food looked really good. Before I took a bite, you know I had to ask who he was at the apartments for.

Trinity, "I don't know what your ordinary flow is but life is full of surprises. I'm just here to add a spark back to yours."

 I laughed a little too hard. He just looked at me, so I got a little nosey.

Trinity, "Now let me ask you this, who do you see when you come over to the apartments? You come over alot so it appears to be someone special."

Y'all he looked at me as he chewed his burger. He started to sip loudly on his mint chocolate shake. All I could think of was whatever lie he tell; I'm just going to follow him one day to see for myself. He still too fine. It was definitely taking too long to answer; I had to break the silence.

Trinity, "So you not gone answer me? Just gone sit there, stare, and make music with your straw? Hello!"

Trey, "I was going to answer, but wanted to see you sweat first."

Trinity, "Boy Fuck You."

Trey laughing, "That's your favorite line huh?"

Now he plays too damn much. At this point my arms are folded and I want to know.

Trinity, "Answer on Playboy."

He sits back in the booth and clears his throat. Whatever he about to say is on him. I'm just gone eat my food and soak up this info he about to spill.

Trey, "Alright but first, What's your real name?"

Trinity, "Trinity."

Trey, "Oh Trinity and Trey. T.T sounds cute huh?"

Yall I laughed so hard because that name is already taken by Donte.

Trinity, "You got jokes I see. Now proceed with the juicy details."

I didn't want to waste no more time.

Trey, "Well my brother lives in building 4A, we are close. As the big bro I'm always popping up.

I almost dropped my fry when he was talking. Something wasn't adding up.

Trinity, "Hold up, that's on the other side of the apartment complex. A long walk a matter of fact. Why don't you park closer? Wooowwww do your brother know about that night?"

Trey, "How else would I see you? Oh yeah, he knows. You really took me out that night. I was late catching my brother so I couldn't sit and tend to the pain."

Trinity, "That don't explain that night for you to park there. If I'm your excuse as to why you park over there."

Trey, "I saw you a few times before."

Trinity, "Stalker vibes much."

Trey, "Something like that."

We laughed but I made sure to keep up a little side eye on him.

As we continued to talk and laugh; I just kept looking him in the eyes. A conversation with Donte was more about him, his brand, having fun being out, but with Trey it was more personal.

Trinity, "You know I prayed for you that night. I didn't want to catch a case."

He laughed but his face got a little serious.

Trey, "So you were my guardian angel that night. I left in a hurry, because I had to go help my brother and his friends. He called me saying they in some mess and when that situation happened with you it made me late. I would've been in a shootout with them. When I got there I was the one rushing everyone to the hospital. My brother got shot in the leg, his friend in the arm. Thank God no one died in that shootout. Some chick set him up; it was a mess."

He grabbed my hand and held it real gently. I just held his back a little tighter; just so he could feel that I'm here for him.

Trey, "Thank you. That shock was awake up call. I'm not in that street life, but how fast I was moving and what could've happened that night to my brother...."

As he tried to talk, I could see the emotions build up. So, I moved from sitting in front of him to sitting next to him. I wrapped my arms around his neck and squeezed him tightly. He loosened up my grip and kissed my arm. He didn't push me away. I slowly released my choke hold I had on him. Just as I returned to my side of the table, he started to leave money for the tab and get up. He reaches out for my hand.

Trey, "I have to go get some things from work and then after I would like to show you something."

Trinity, "Show me what?"

Trey, "It's a surprise."

I just took at his hand and smiled.

# Chapter 7
# You Work Where

We ended up at a recreation center. I know it would be better to tell y'all the conversation, but it would've been too long. So, I am going to summarize it. Come to find out he is a teacher. He has his OWN non-profit recreational center. He loves the kids. I love my Gerbil Maxine. Don't get me wrong I love kids, but I will check a kid real quick. Those you can't tell nothing to, smart mouth kids.... well, my mouth can get smart back too in the most loving way. We went inside and met some of his mentees. He grabbed me some shorts and T-shirt with his Recreation Logo. He said I may need it for later, but I don't know why. Also, I still don't have any panties on, so it's not that much changing I'm going to do. It was hard getting him out of there. Everyone wanted to show him something or ask something.

Honestly, he looked happy. So, when we finally left, we ended up at Lake Rabun. It was so beautiful and peaceful. On the way we stopped for drinks and snacks. I trusted him enough to go but wasn't crazy enough to not be packing. I had my taser, pepper spray, and switch blade with me. I made him get out the car as I went into the backseat to change clothes. As I ripped open the packaging these clothes was new and of good quality. I was impressed. When I got out the car, he was leaning on the hood drinking out of a juice box. I walked up to him.

Trinity, "So you got your brother watching my apartment?"

Trey, "Wait a minute (with a smile) not watching your apartments, but maybe keep an eye out.

Trinity, "Stalker! You got me out here to hurt me. Think again I will fuck you up!"

Trey, "So aggressive, I believe you."

I was definitely not going to enjoy my time with him if I keep popping off, so I calmed down. I figured to just live in the moment. I turned and looked at the beautiful view. Trey was staring at me from behind. Yes, my booty was eating up them shorts.

Trey, "Come here and let me see you model that expensive designer outfit you have on."

I did exactly that but made sure I did some prison poses with a little two step. That really made him laugh. Somehow the juice from his juice box came out his nose. I laughed and took some napkins to playfully wipe his nose.

Trinity, "So it was that funny huh?"

Trey, "Yes you were that funny. It's getting late, let me get you back home."

I thought he was mad that he embarrassed himself, but when we got in the car; he gently held my hand and kissed it. Twice y'all. I hope he didn't think that he was going to get some tonight. Now that's a big NO.

You know what I said I was going to chill out. He hasn't come across me with no crazy behavior, so I need to calm down. Usually, you are looking for the guy to be wanting some from you but that's not the case so far. I definitely need to chill. I'm not gone lie everything was on point today. The scenery, emotions, and being treated nice. Trey was a gentleman, and he loved the kids. To that note I love my Gerbil Maxine.

## Chapter 8
## The Ride Home

On the ride home we talked about our favorite foods, families, and hobbies. Nothing was pressured at all. Everything was flowing organically between us. So as he was telling me another funny joke; I could not stop laughing. My head went back then as we stopped at the red light; I leaned forward to catch my breath. As I sat up and looked out my window for a quick second. Guess who was in the car next to us. At the motherfucking red light. Bitch ass Donte with Sydney coming up from his lap, wiping slob from her mouth. The way he drove off so fast, I knew damn well they didn't see me. That Great Value looking ass nigga. Even though he was labeled as my friend, we all knew he was more to me. He knew I'm cool with Sydney, and he got her slurping him up like that. She knew I liked him that way. They both are wrong.

My whole energy changed so quick. I was really hurt. Fuck that nigga. I'm glad I didn't sleep with his ass, and that ....that Bitch. I considered her a friend. Trey was still trying to keep having fun. When I didn't respond he looked over towards me. I had a nasty look on my face. I couldn't help it. My feelings were hurt. I didn't hear about them or anything. I saw it right before my eyes, at a fucking red light. Silence hit the car for a good five minutes. Thank God we were close to my apartments. I just wanted to go home and cry. Not even plot my revenge just yet just cry. I stared out the window waiting for him to turn towards my building. I was going to jump out and go straight to my apartment. No words or anything; I was that hurt. When he pulled into the parking space of my building, I started to do just that. As I opened the car door, he gently grabbed my hand. I sat back down in the car seat and looked out the window as he held my hand.

Trey, " What's wrong? We went from laughing to silence."

Trinity, "I just saw some stuff that pissed me off."

Trey, "What?"

Trinity, "That green mustang had my frien...I mean a recent ex friend of mines, slobbing on the guy I was hanging out with on a regular. Me and him was just friends and we all hang out together. They both wrong."

I know I told Trey a lot, but I was hurt. He really sat there and listened. After a great day with him, I hate I saw that stuff. He gently took my other hand and caressed it. I forgot this man had my other hand.

Trey, "That's fucked up. I know what they did was fucked up and at a red light. They way you saw that is a 1 in a million chance. Look to that as a sign. You are too smart and beautiful to let those birds get you down. They did you a favor and showed you who they really are. They are straight trash."

Trinity looking up smiling, "Now Trey (wiping away a tear) you definitely just cheered me up. Thank you.

We sat in silence for a brief moment.

Trinity, "They were my circle. Now I have to find new people. That's some Bull Shit. I'm going to beat her ass and key his car.

Trey, "Well damn."

Trinity, "Just answer the phone if I call you from jail. What's your number again?"

Trey shaking his head, "It's not worth it. Trust me. Cutt your losses and make a new circle. You know with people like me and other females that see your worth from the start.

Trinity, "Thank you Dr. Trey. I appreciate your words of encouragement.

Trey, "No problem, please don't go do anything crazy. I don't take collect calls.... I'm just joking but go look in the mirror and see your worth like I do. You the Shit sugar honey Iced Tea." He started laughing.

Trinity, "I'm all that and a bag of chips; thank you." I couldn't stop smiling. He really had a way with words.

As I left his car, I felt better. I still wanted to beat Sydney ass and key Donte car. It was the principle of how they played me. I'm not going to do it though. I have too much to lose. Instead, I sent a group message to them.

# Chapter 9
# The Group Message

Trinity:
I saw Ya'll at the red light. I hope the head from Sydney was good. Both ya'll hoes lost a good friend.

7:05PM

Donte:
Sydney Who? I wasn't getting no head from no Sydney.

7:09PM

Trinity:
Nigga you lying, but I'm too grown for childish games.
I saw ya'll so whatever BYE 🖕

7:12PM

Donte:
That hoe don't mean shit. Don't lose the type of friendship we have over no dumb hoe.

7:19PM

Trinity:
I thought you didn't know NO HOE NAMED SYDNEY?

7:23PM

Donte:
That hoe came by saying you was in a puppy love over me, and she knew the kind of woman I need. She needed a ride to her car from the shop. You know Your my T.T. Don't let no hear say come between us.

7:33PM

Sydney:
So I don't mean shit? You selling me out to this bitch! Ok Cool BET THAT Donte

7:43PM

Trinity:
Oh now Hoes Speak. Thanks Sydney for showing me how a fake ass bitch you are. Slick dissing me on the low. Thanks Donte for showing me how easy you are with these HOES. Ya'll can have each other. Oh, and Sydney did you tell Donte you were on day 8 of your antibiotics? My bad catching Syphilis wasn't on your list huh Donte. Get tested old friend. Hoeing don't pay huh? Doctor bills going to be out that ass huh? I mean mouth LMAO

7:49PM

Donte:
sydney You Bitch

7:53PM

Sydney:
Fuck you Donte! Trinity I thought I could Trust you. You gone see me bitch!

7:59PM

Trinity:
Sydney you was slick dissing me. That puppy love shit and then I saw you sucking his dick at the red light. I thought You was my friend, but you was really an OPP. Keep your other secrets. Now see me on that.

8:03PM

Donte:
Sydney you ain't gone lay a hand on her. Trust me.

8:13PM

Trinity:
Both of ya'll go see a Doctor Blocked Ass Hoes.

8:23PM

8:25PM

I did just that, before Sydney could respond; I blocked they asses. That felt so good. I know Trey said to know my worth and I know myself. I'm very petty when provoked. That whole thing provoked me. Yes, I may have been wrong for telling Donte that Sydney had Syphilis, but at this point I can't take it back. I will in the future leave gracefully from a situation without telling anyone business. I'm working on myself.

Am I the only one who notice how Donte lied, but still took up for me. He technically wasn't my man. We all hung out with each other. I was under this man each time. So there was no confusion of together without a title. Just Dumb. I don't even want to know how long Sydney was plotting against me. That will definitely make my head hurt. I said what I said, they said what they said, and now I'm on my way to start healing from this situation. I do expect to get into a fight from behind this so mentally I'm preparing myself.

A week has passed, and I haven't been bothered by that drama. Although Sydney and Donte were still on my block list; The only person who reached out was Donte Uncle. I did not respond back. Trey messaged me a few times, but I haven't responded back to him either. I don't want to hear any turn the other cheek, cheer up mantra. I'm sulking at the moment, and I'm fine with that.

# Chapter 10
# Dude Crazy

This week was going by well. I really indulge in other areas of my life. I talked to the other females I met. They were cool and on a whole different vibe. They were on some level up, travel, generational wealth type stuff. I didn't mention the Donte, Sydney situation though. So, for the most part everything was lighthearted. Right now, it's Saturday around 10:30pm and raining really hard. I hear a knock on my door. I'm not expecting any company, so I had my pistol ready. It wasn't a bad neighborhood, but I just wanted to stay ready. The beef with Sydney and Donte was still fresh so you never know. Before I opened the door, I look out the peep hole to see who it was. Speaking of the devil, it was Donte at my door. Soaking wet. I didn't know to open the door or just act like I wasn't home.

Stupidly I opened the door. Word of advice don't ever open the door; let they ass stand there or call the cops. So, he was soaking wet. I stood there with my pistol visibly in my hand; just so he knew I mean business.

Trinity, "Why are you here?"

Donte, "I'm sorry I know I hurt your feelings, and the situation was messed up. I do care about you; I miss being around you. Your still my friend."

Trinity, "Friends come and go. We are too old for the back and forth. I heard what you said but actions speak louder than words. My actions are to let you go."

Donte, "I had to sort out my feelings, get tested, and handle some shit. I needed to sort out my actions."

Trinity, "I glad you had a come to Jesus moment, but that's between you and Sydney not me."

He lowered his head and stepped closer in my doorway. I stepped aside slightly to not get wet from the rain. No matter how fine a guy is, I'm not going to be dumb for him. I was about to kick him out and go make popcorn. Dang, I shouldn't have opened the door.

Donte, "She's Pregnant."

Trinity, "Hold up, how long have ya'll been fucking? I know damn well this ain't happened in just a week from no head! If ya'll been fucking why haven't ya'll said nothing. We been hanging out together. The whole time I was on you and You was on ME! We ain't fucked or nothing but WTF! Ya'll too shady. GET OUT!"

Donte, "Just listen. It's been a few months. I lied on the text, because I was pissed. I'm sorry. I didn't think I wasn't going to lose you. She told me things like you was for the streets and using me. I would've been made you my woman. I'm sorry."

Trinity, "Nigga we grown. We talked about how we feel about each other. You should've come straight to me. I told her all the times I wanted you and she downplayed it like you was a hoe. You let someone get in your head that's not what a real man does. That bitch PREGNANT! Ya'll was fucking for months and in front of her you were all on me. Ya'll some Fucking weirdos."

Donte, "I'm a man regardless of the situation lets' get that straight. All those times I held you or even hugged you longer that was me wanting you. That's my fault for playing that game and I learned a hard lesson. Don't let us end like this."

Trinity, "You know what FUCK BOTH OF YA'LL! That baby is innocent, but I'm not going to be involved in ya'll mess. You ain't the man I thought you were. Playing some childish ass game. We ain't 10 or 15 years old. Your excuses are lame. We didn't fuck so we have no ties together."

Trinity, "You wasn't my nigga, I just liked you. You got burned by a bitch I only knew for a few months. Congratulations Fatherhood looks so good on you. Now get out of my doorway and don't come back."

## Chapter 11

## You got me Fucked Up

Donte looked at me up and down. He licked his tired ass great value lips and jumped at me like he was going to slap me. I don't know who the fuck he thought I was, but my pistol hasn't left my side. I'm glad I didn't fall even harder for him. He definitely showed me who he really was. Now I know my mouth can come off too blunt at times, but oh well the truth is the truth. He tried to get closer, and I made sure my pistol raised right between his eyes.

Donte, "You ain't nothing, but a groupie anyway. Sydney was right you self righteous BITCH."

Trinity, "Sydney Boy get your begging ass, std fan club having ass out of my house!"

As we were screaming at each other the thunder was getting louder. I tried to quickly slam my door on him shut but he pushed his weight on the door. Remind you this is all because I stopped our friendship. Dude Crazy.

Imagine if I slept with him. He would've been crazier. I never lowered my gun on him. Trinity, "Get out my house Donte, before this bullet leave you in a body bag!"

Yes ya'll it was to that extreme. Do not underestimate anyone, because the moment you tell them no; they become a whole new person. At that moment there wasn't a sexy man standing in front of me. There was hate in his eyes, his body was tensed, and his fist was bawled up. I could feel like he was going to try to hurt me. His body language was the reason I kept my gun pointed on him. As the rain came down harder, he lunged out towards me. The gun fell out of my hand, and slide towards the front door. I scrambled towards the gun, but he caught me by the waist. He kicked the door closed and started squeezing me tightly. I fought and wiggled as much as I could as he dragged me towards my couch. He was strong, so I had to come up with a plan quick.

I relaxed my body, took a deep breath, then head butted his ass. He jerked back and loosened his grip. I was not about to be raped, so I ran fast as I could towards my gun. I grabbed it just in time and took it off safety. I shot at his head but missed. The bullet went through my window as he picked up my favorite chair. He slung it so hard at me it shattered against the wall. I shot another round, and it went towards his leg. He let out a scream as he tried to limp towards me with a vengeance. The thunder didn't mask the noise that was coming from my apartment. Someone was beating hard on my door; out of breath I opened it. As I opened it that didn't stop Donte for still trying to come after me. Thank God it was the police. My neighbors heard all the noise and called them. I have only been living here a few months and never saw police at my apartments. With the door opened the police guns was pointed at me.

## Chapter 12

## What Just Happened?

Police, "Put the Gun DOWN!"

Donte, "That Bitch Shot Me!"

I lowered my gun and they started to arrest me. Arrest ME of all people. My hands were cuffed as they sat me down on my couch. I didn't know that blood was pouring from my head from head butting Donte. The cops called the paramedics, while handcuffing Donte. They started asking questions as the paramedics arrived. The fact that I was coherent enough to answer their questions, the paramedics started to work on Donte. They patched him up quick. Now ain't that a bitch, my aim was off. I just grazed that nigga leg. It didn't even go through his leg. I'm more pissed that after all this my fucking aim have been off. When all this is over, I'm definitely going back to the gun range.

As the cops finished talking to the neighbors, and hearing both our sides of what happened; they ruled it was self-defense. The cops uncuffed me so the paramedics could take me to the hospital.

Paramedic, "Mam we need to take you to the hospital to see how far your head wound goes."

I walked with the paramedic to the ambulance. As I was walking the police started asking me will I press charges. YES THE FUCK I AM! He is definitely not going to get away with what he did to me tonight.

Trey walks past the police taking Donte to their car. Looking around he rushed to me. I notice he was holding a small box with holes in it. It had a big blue bow on top. It was still pouring down raining as everything started to get blurry to me.

Trey, "Trinity what's going on? Is everything ok?"

Trinity, "Trey, umm."

Ya'll, I passed the fuck out. Literally laid out. Trey tried to catch me while the paramedic yelled to her team to get the stretcher. Everything went black. What happened to me? I could hear people but couldn't open my eyes. It was like I drifted away or something. Did I hit him that hard and got a concussion? I could only think. My Monday through Thursdays be so good, but my weekends be some bullshit these last few weeks. I finally could open my eyes and saw my mom and dad by my side. I was at the hospital that I currently work at. I'm glad that I forgot to put in my 2 weeks' notice.

Mom, "Thank God your awake. Baby how are you feeling?"

Dad, "Let her ease into opening her eyes up. Baby we are taking you home once you get better."

As they started talking, I could feel my blood pressure rising. The monitors did too, because they started to beep loudly.

Mom, "Cliff run! Go get the Doctor!"

As my Dad started to run out the room, the nurse came in. I worked with her a few times, so I know she good at what she does. She checked my monitors. My throat was so dry I could barely speak. As I reached for the water my head started to hurt. The nurse had to help me with my water because I was in so much pain, but why? Trey walked in with two cups of coffee for my Mom and Dad. As my Dad thanked him, they stepped out with the nurse to ask her my progress. My mom was pouring me more water and talking about taking me back home. Moving back to South Caroline, I be damned. This was a minor setback to a major comeback. I just had to figure out what happened. My mom stepped out the room to get an update. Trey came back in the room and smiled at me. This man has really been around in my time of need. I'm confused and grateful that he is here at the same time.

Trey, "You really be in some shit huh?"

I tried to laugh, but I was sore, and my throat wasn't ready to talk. He saw that and just kept talking.

Trey, "Your parents are sweet. Your mom just stopped crying and your Dad been screaming she knows how to shoot better than that. I'm glad your ok."

Trinity (sounding muffled), "What happened?"

Trey sat on the edge of my hospital bed and looked at me. He then pulled out his phone and just stared at it.

Trinity (Trying to get louder but it wasn't but a whisper), "What happened?"

Trey, "Donte injected you with a date rape drug. You had a bad reaction to it."

A tear fell down my face. That's why he squeezed me so hard. That's why he didn't run for that gun first. This nigga planned on hurting me from the beginning.

Trinity, "How long have I been here?"

Trey, "Four days."

Trinity (coughing), "Four days? Am I ok?"

Trey, "Everything is getting back to normal. Your body just needed to respond to the medication, and you needed to wake up."

Before I could ask another question; my mom and dad walked in.

Mom, "Baby I'm so proud of you. You're so strong."

Dad, "We should've never let you come up here. These fools almost got my baby. You know how to shoot!"

Mom, "Cliff!"

Dad, "I'm sorry Trin. It's a blessing you are here. Once you get well your cousin Peewee can come back and get your things. Georgia my ass. You want to move somewhere move down the street."

For the next few days, I ignored my parents when it came to the talk of me moving back home.

# Chapter 13

# Your friend huh?

While I was getting released from the hospital my mother started asking questions.

Mom, "Who is Trey to you?"

Trinity, "Well Trey....He is just a friend."

Mom, "Just a friend. Have ya'll you know?"

Remind ya'll I will be 27 years old in a month. If I wanted to have sex I would, but my body is precious and I'm not giving that up to just anybody. I don't care if I like them or not. Why my mom so pressed on that part I never know.

Trinity, "Mom... NO! Why would you ask?"

Mom, "He called us on your phone, the night everything happened. He has been by your side every day until you woke up. Your father seems to like him. They cleaned up your apartment and fixed the window. He's doing a lot to be just a friend. He seems like a good person though."

Trinity, "Yes he has always been a good person to me."

I started to change the subject. After everything went on, I didn't even think how my parents knew what happened or where I was. How did he even get into my phone. Yes, I'm glad my parents are here but Trey a little too good. Something is up.

Trinity, "Mom what did the apartment complex say?"

Mom, "Well since there is no mention of your registered gun it wasn't too bad on you. They were just glad you were safe. Now that asshole you were dealing with... was he your boyfriend?"

Trinity, "No he was just a friend that turned on me when I didn't want to be his friend no more."

Mom, "Pay attention to the people you deal with. Wolves can wear the best sheep as clothing."

Trinity, "I don't think you said that right."

Mom, "I said what I said."

We both started laughing. As we got into the car I looked around for my Dad.

Trinity, "Mom where's Dad?"

Mom, "He's at your apartment getting it ready for you. Are you sure you don't want to come home?"

Trinity, "Yes Mom, I'm a 100 percent sure.

When I got home it was balloons and flowers everywhere. All I could do was smile. Trey was there with the same box that had a big blue ribbon on it. I drunk a protein drink while my parents and Trey at a home cook meal. My apartment didn't feel like the memory of me and Donte fighting; but more like family enjoying their selves. I was getting tired, so my parents started to leave to take that drive back to South Carolina. My Dad made Trey promise to take care of me and then there was just us. Trey cleaned up quietly, then sat down next to me.

He handed me the box that felt like it was vibrating. I opened it and to my surprise it was a male Gerbil. He had a card attached to him that said Kyle Barker. I cried ya'll in pain and all.

Trey, "Maxine Shaw needed Kyle Barker."

He started wiping away my tears. Where did this man come from? He gets my logic, he's patient, kind, loves kids, and fine. I'm myself with him and he has been by my side through the unimaginable. I couldn't say anything I just looked at him.

# Chapter 14

## And Then He Said

Trey, "I know you been through a lot these last few days, well weeks really. When your father and I cleaned up your apartment; I knew it may have been too soon to come back here."

Trinity, "Did my Dad find my ..."

He cut me off and laughed.

Trey, "I found your little friend, need some new batteries huh?"

As he laughed, I placed Kyle in his new cage with Maxine.

Trinity, "I'm going to ignore that. I have fresh batteries ready for action."

Trey, "Well you keep them on standby until you fully recover."

Trinity, "Whatever."

Trey, "If you feel up to it; do you want to come stay at my house tonight?"

I took a moment to think about his offer. It would feel nice to feel safer tonight.

Trinity, "Wow this would be my first time there. I would like to stay the night, but no funny business."

He smiled and stood up. He asked to help me pack, but I was only going to be there for one night. We managed to pack for days. I gave Maxine and Kyle some extra water and food, then headed to Trey house. I was exhausted so I slept the whole way there. Red Flag #1. I never been there so how do I really know where I'm going? I trusted him, but I also listened to the little voice in the back of my mind to bring my gun and taser. I slipped that in my bag when he wasn't looking. Even though this man has been heaven to me; I still wanted some other protection. I woke up as we were stopping at this gorgeous home.

Trinity, "Where are we?"

Trey, "My home."

Trinity, "Where?"

Trey, "Buckhead."

He gets out the car and as I looked past him; I could see the gorgeous view of the city. I didn't want to look like I was in disbelief, so I kept my cool. I'm not saying he couldn't have money, but he said he was a teacher, and he did own a non-profit recreational center. My head was hurting trying to connect the dots to how he gets his money; so I just went with the flow. We walked into a gorgeous semi glass house. When I saw the pool I just fell in love with the layout even more. Red Flag #2, I stopped paying attention to Trey and was focused on the layout of the house. Trey turned around and started talking. I didn't know what he was saying, I was focused on the house.

Trey, "Are you hungry?" All you ate well drank was a protein drink. I can make you some soup."

Trinity looking "I can eat."

It was late at night around 11 something. I still had a little energy from taking a nap on the drive up to his home. He watched me as I sat down on his bar stool. The look on my face must have told him what I was thinking so he looked away. I didn't want him to feel awkward and wanted to enjoy my time here with him, so I took a deep breath and shifted in my seat. Instead of looking at him with curiosity, I looked at him with admiration. He turned on some light instrumental music and became my chef. This man was making me some chicken and dumplings. The food was smelling so good. He caught a few glimpses of me smiling at him without saying a word. As he fed me a few pieces of chicken that was done cooking; my taste buds were in love. He can season some food; before he was finish, I walked away to explore. I made my way outdoors towards the pool. In the night sky the lights made the water in the pool more mesmerizing.

I was on some strong med right now, so I had to get a hold of myself and snap back into reality. I was going to enjoy my time here, but while I'm outside I'm also going to map out my exits. I'm not stupid, Trey is fine, owns a non - profit, has a fancy house, always know the right thing to say, and he can season up some chicken. Come on ya'll I didn't think Donte was dumb crazy, so I'm just being cautious. I looked around the backyard just in case I needed to run. I saw a few heavy rocks and I placed them behind a nearby tree. It looks like I was hiding eggs for an Easter egg hunt in the dark. I heard Trey call my name. So I started walking around to the front door. When we came in earlier, I saw the alarm code as he put it in. I wrote it down on a piece of small paper while I was sitting at the table in his kitchen. I placed the paper under his welcome mat at his front door. I wasn't playing. I'm not going to argue with anyone this time I'm going ghost. I learned my lesson.

I was making my way back towards the back yard, before I could get too far.

Trey, "Exploring the house?"

I jumped and said the first thing that came to my mind.

Trinity, "Yes, it's beautiful. Your wife must not be at home?"

He laughed and gestured me to follow him towards the kitchen.

Trey, "No I don't have a wife. I know you may have a lot of questions, but I promise you in the morning I will answer all of them."

We made it to the kitchen and as I opened my mouth to object to that, he gently shoved a dumpling into my mouth. Oh man you guys he can cook. I shut up though and ate all my food. He grabbed some blankets, and we went to his living room. He turned the tv on low and I leaned my body on his. He gently wrapped his arms around me, and I fell asleep in his embrace. I had to admit he was perfect.

# Chapter 15
# The Gator Shoes

The morning started with the sound of his phone ringing. Instead of grabbing his phone first he kissed my forehead. I was still in his arms as his phone rang again. He got up off the couch and answered his call. As he was walking through the house, I could faintly hear his conversation. I started to sit up and put on my shoes. I don't even know where he put my overnight bag at. At this point I'm standing looking around to see where my bag was; he walks back in the living room.

Trey, "Good Morning, you don't have to get up. You could lay back down. I have to go and handle somethings really quick. It won't even take an hour. If your thirsty or hungry there is water, juice, food in the fridge. Are you ok to stay?"

Trinity, "Yes, I'm good."

Why did I say that? He was being so nice, and I actually slept good sleeping on him. Dang why I didn't say anything about my overnight bag. So, my mind went back to curiosity towards him and yes, I'm going to snoop around his house. You can say I'm wrong but hey my excuse is I'm looking for my overnight bag. I walked him to the door and watched him leave the driveway. I made sure he was down the street and out of sight before I closed the door. I went to each room and open the door. They were the typical rooms so far until I made it to his bedroom. He had a small office in it with papers all on it. I saw his bank statements, and everything was good. Great actually, he had money. Crazy amount of money. Red Flag #3 what the fuck is going on? I went from cussing and fighting an ex-friend; to going through another friend shit. I was definitely losing it and need to fix my life fast. I know I'm worthy of great things, but I got a lot of questions to ask Trey.

The more I went through his things the more my curiosity of figuring out who Trey really was heightened. I left everything on his desk alone and made my way to his closet. It was neat and clean okay, but the smell was strong. I smelled some of his clothes and they were sprayed with different colognes. I stood in his closet and just was done; this man is perfect and it's just Gods way of sending me my miracle man. I'm done being suspicious and I'm letting my guard down when he gets back. I was about to walk out and go see what he has in the fridge to make breakfast for the both of us. This would be my way of showing my appreciation for him. I looked down and almost screamed. I thought it was something coming to get me from all this snooping I been doing. Since it didn't move when I kicked at it, I looked closer. It was these alligator shoes with eyes on it. These pair were about $900 just for some loafers.

Let me tell you I know the price, because my father cussed out my uncle over it. Long story short, my uncle didn't pay his mortgage for that month, bought the shoes, then asked my father to help with his bills. Crazy stuff, but back to my story. I picked up the shoes just to walk a tab bit in them, when a door flung open. My heart raced so fast, because I thought it was Trey. My intuition was right something was up with this man.

## Chapter 16
## Photos Don't Lie

As I put the Gator shoes back down exactly how I found them. The door suddenly closed. I picked the shoes back up and the door opened again. Before I stepped into the secret room, I got one of Treys beat up old looking shoes and placed them in the doorway, so it won't shut completely. Walking into the room made my suspicions of him right; he was crazy. There were pictures of people on the wall, guns laid out, and cameras everywhere. I literally walked into a scene off a movie. Why has everyone around me been crazy? Why am I attracting these types of people? I'm leaving. I'm like fuck finding that overnight bag and calling me an Uber. I plan on walking down the street to a main road or something because this is not it. He ain't about to get me. I picked up one of his guns as I headed out the secret room just for protection.

Walking out I stumbled on box on the floor. It was pictures old pictures of me and Sydney hanging out; also pictures of Donte with other women. This man was fucking crazy, and I knew it. He was too good to be true. I heard his car pull back up. I quickly snatched one of the old pictures he took of me and Sydney; then kicked his old shoe from the secret door. It was not enough time to hide so I pointed the gun straight at the closet door. I will not miss this time. I could hear him whistle walking through the front door. He has the nerve to whistle not knowing I know he crazy. He gently calls my name. I didn't answer as I tried to come out the closet and tip toe towards the bedroom door to close and lock it. I kept the gun pointing straight at the door. His tone gets even more worried as he calls my name again. I hear him sitting bags down on the counter. I'm trying to figure out a plan. I remember the front door is past the kitchen, the pool area is facing the kitchen. Damn.

Every exit was near that damn kitchen. I guess I have to shoot my way out of this one. I notice he stopped calling my name and the house was quiet. As I walked towards the hallway my shoes squeaked. I tried to slip them off, but he heard me. I could hear him walk towards me so I ran as fast as I could. He was quicker, because he slid right in front of the door. I pulled the gun directly towards his head.

Trinity, "Move Psycho!"

Trey, "Woah calm down! What's going on?"

I started to back up to run for the pool area. I wasn't fazed by him being by the door. I already mapped out my escape routes earlier.

Trinity, "Your Fucking Crazy and I won't miss this time!"

Trey demeanor changed; but not like how Donte did. He calmly spoked as the gun was still pointed at him.

Trey, "Tell me what happened?"

I threw the old picture of me and Sydney at him. It fell on the floor. He picked it up keeping his eye on me. He let out a sigh of relief like it wasn't nothing bad. Dude a weirdo I need to get out.

Trey, "Let me explain. At least give me that. You don't have to lower the gun. Just hear me out. I followed you and the people you were around a few times after that night I officially met you. I know it looks crazy, but I couldn't get you out of my mind since that night. I had to find out more about you. I'm sorry this is all scaring you.

Trinity, "You got me fucked up. What you think a sob story gone help you like that think again. You on some serial killa type shit and I'm not gone be one of your victims. I already called the cops."

I didn't call the cops just yet but that didn't seem to bother him at all. He just laughed and slowly walked closer to me. I shot a bullet that went past his head.

He was on another level kind of crazy, because he didn't flinch.

Trey, "Look let me show you, ask me anything and I will be honest with you. You missed on purpose; you're not trying to shoot me. Trust me I only want to protect you. Ask me anything."

Trinity, "How I know what's the truth? Your already sneaking around following me. Who the fuck are you?"

Trey, "I haven't lied to you. I just wanted to make sure you are who you say you are."

Trinity, "Your Crazy just move so I can leave."

Trey, "Yes I am, but I won't ever hurt you."

Hold on this man just admit he was crazy...At that moment I believed him. He hasn't really shown me anything hurtful. Yes, my suspicions were right yes, he's crazy, but can I handle that? I don't know, he still could be lying, but he was stalking me. I lowered the gun down and asked...

# Chapter 17
# Who Are You?

Trinity, "What do you really do?"

Trey, "I am a government private detective. I do run and own the recreation center as well.

Trinity, "So you already knew my parents' number?"

Trey, "Well it was easy for me to find, but yes. Please don't be scared."

Trinity, "Are you going to try to control me?"

Trey, "No, I am in love with who you are."

Trinity, "In love?"

Trey, "Yes, that's how it got to this extreme. I'm sorry you found out like this."

Trinity, "No secrets between us, tell me everything and I mean everything with proof."

Well ya'll he did just that. He provided proof with bank statements, phone passwords everything. He was who he said he was. I stayed with him that day.

That night I found my overnight bag in the coat closet. I took 2 pain pills as he cooked dinner. I kept his gun by my side, and he never tried to take it from me.  After we ate the pain pill started to kick in. He sat on one end of the couch, and I sat on the other end holding his gun on my lap. I'm not going to blame my hormones or this loopy feeling from those pain pills; I actually wanted him. I got up, sat the gun to the side and walked towards him. He just stared at me. At this point I was the aggressor. As I sat down on his lap facing him, he gently pulled me to the side of him.

Trey, "You don't have to do this. Also, you need time to heal."

Before he could say anything else I got back on his lap and started kissing him. This time he didn't stop me. His body seemed like he was relieved he could touch me. Before you scream no I didn't. Yes, THE FUCK I DID! I let that man make love to me and I enjoyed every moment.

That was the best thing I have done these last few weeks. He was so gentle, patient, and hit every spot imaginable. That night was one to remember.

# Chapter 18

# Update...

So, lets fast forward to my present. I'm 6 months pregnant with our 3rd child. Trey and I are married, and we haven't left each other side since that night. Let me answer a few questions, no he is not controlling, yes, I have my freedom, and yes, he is still crazy nosey. Well, that's his job. All in all, I am truly happy. He has shown me time and time again that he has me and our children best interest at heart. I couldn't ask for a better man, father, husband, and provider. The kids and I don't want for anything, and we have everything. I still work at that same hospital I started at after that incident. I have some great friends and definitely ready to have this baby any day now. I know it started off crazy, but it's going beautifully now. Now if ya'll was in my shoes would ya'll say I'm crazy if you knew the ending was a good one?

Let me give you all the updates before I let you go. Remember Sydney? I caught her in the store after I had my 2nd child Maxine. I was buying some diapers when she stopped me in the aisle trying to speak. I started throwing pacifiers at her telling her to suck on that then started punching her. That beef wasn't over until I fought her. I did just that and won; so now it's over. Oh, and that baby Donte said she was pregnant with wasn't even his. So boom, I won in the end of that drama. Maybe I can tell ya'll the story of what happened after I had my first child Trent. Trey ex came to the hospital trying to steal our baby. No I got a good one; the story from the day of our wedding. One of his brother enemies tried to kidnap my braidmaids. Its so many things to tell ya'll and so little time.

Trey walked in with two kids in his arms.

Trey, "Hey baby ready to go eat?"

Trinity, "I'm ready just one moment let me close this chapter."

Bye ya'll some Hibachi food is calling my name.....

# Know that YOU are Worthy
# &
# Grab a copy of the

Ease Your Mind Journal Series Everyday life Struggles the Basics

Join the conversation at
**WinnieUmbrellaPublishing.com**
for your Next favorite Book

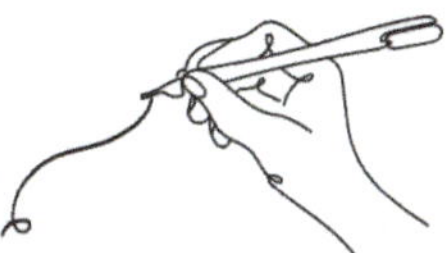